CARLY TRIES NEW FOODS

by Katrina Liu

Illustrated by
Bella Ansori

ISBN 979-8-89111-020-5

This is Carly. Carly never backed down from a new adventure.

She's tried skiing, snorkeling and even rock climbing!

She especially loved adventures with her best friend, Olivia.

In fact, the only thing Carly wasn't adventurous with was food.

Carly was what some people might call a "very picky eater."

Carly only ate from a short list: breads, rice, buttered noodles, mashed potatoes, cookies, cake and of course her favorite, French fries!

Carly could eat them every day if she'd had her way!

"Why don't you try some eggs?" Mom asked at breakfast.
"Or some bacon?" Dad offered.

Carly refused. She'd stick with pancakes and the occasional waffle.

At lunchtime, her friends often shared foods so they could try new things.

"Have some grapes!" Olivia said.

"Would you like to try some sushi?" another asked.

Carly shook her head as she ate only the bread from her sandwich.

At dinner, Carly's parents prepared baked chicken, mashed potatoes and broccoli.

"Just try a bite!" said Dad.

Carly ate the mashed potatoes, then, when no one was watching, she gave the chicken to her dog, Bun-bun.

It was the day of Olivia's birthday sleepover party.
Carly arrived in her new french fry pajamas.

Olivia greeted her with a big hug.
"Wait until you see what we've set up!"

"It's my around-the-world party! We've got games and music from all over the world. Best of all, we have yummy foods from many different countries!" Olivia said with excitement.

"Isn't it amazing?!" said Olivia.

Carly's eyes widened at a table filled with so many strange and colorful foods.

Ratatouille
France

Peking Duck
China

Samosas
India

Boba milk tea
Taiwan

Paella
Spain

Bibimbap
Korea

Gumbo
New Orleans

Lumpia
Philippines

"Do you have anything less colorful?
Like buttered noodles or french fries?"
Carly asked.

Olivia's face fell. "I'm sorry.
We don't have any of those things."

"That's okay!" Carly said, trying to smile.
"I'll just wait for the birthday cake."

"Oh. Actually, we're not having birthday cake,"
Olivia informed. "We're having Japanese
mochi with sweet red bean for dessert."

Carly's smile dropped. There was nothing here for her to eat, and it was a sleepover. That meant she would go hungry all night!

Everyone at the party danced and played games.
Carly tried to join in, but the more she ran around,
the more her stomach began to rumble.

"Dinner!"
Olivia's mom announced.

Sounds of
"Yum!" and **"Mmmm!"**
filled the room.

Olivia noticed Carly with an empty plate.
"Just think of it as one of our adventures
together!" Olivia told her encouragingly.

Carly did enjoy going on adventures with Olivia. And of course, she loved her best friend. She didn't want her to feel bad, especially not on her birthday.

"Try it, Carly! You can do it!" her friends cheered.

Hesitantly, Carly took a tiny spoonful of seafood paella and started to chew.

Amazing flavors and textures danced around in her mouth.
"Mmmmmm!" she exclaimed, spooning in another bite.

Carly began to take bites of the other foods. Every dish had a wonderful and unique flavor, like nothing she'd ever tasted!

"WOW! I never knew food could taste this good! Why didn't anyone tell me to try them?" she asked.

Everyone burst into laughter. "Oh, Carly!" Olivia giggled.
"You really are one of a kind!"

For Mina, Leah and Eli

The inspiration for everything I do.

About the Author

Katrina Liu is an American-born Chinese/Taiwanese mom and indie author living in San Francisco, CA. She was inspired by her children to create books with Asian-American characters where they can see themselves reflected in. Her mission is to add more Asian representation into the world of children's books and normalize Asian characters in everyday stories. She's also passionate about dual-language learning and has published several bilingual books in Chinese and English for non-native speakers.

Check out these other titles by Katrina Liu

For more books visit
www.lycheepress.com

24504947R00019